Third wheel

I was all up in my favorite night club looking for a curvy babe to dance with and avoiding the skinny babes. An hour in and I was having no luck until I felt someone behind me rubbing my shoulders and whispering in my ears, hey stud do you want to dance.

I turned around and jackpot, my favorite a curvy white girl smiling at me. I said of course I would love to dance with you. I took the goddess in my arms, and we started dancing while smiling at each other. She said my name is Heather and I said pleasure to meet you lady with the dangerous curves. She smiled at me and kissed me on the cheek.

A few minutes later we were glued to each other and grinding on each other. I thought I definitely dig her, pretty blonde with curves. I felt my erection make an appearance and Heather held me tighter. I knew she liked it, that's when I reached down and felt her glorious big ass.

I said damn you have a really nice big ass. Heather said thank you stud reaching between us to stroke my cock then she said you have a nice big black cock too. I replied thank you Heather that's when she pulled me against the wall and kissed the hell out of me. I was very happy to reciprocate her passion. I massaged and squeezed her juicy booty as we kissed for a long time.

When we came up for air, Heather turned around and pulled me on her sexy big booty. I held her hips and worked my hard cock into her big white booty. Damn it felt amazing grinding on her big ass. I massaged her sweet white thighs as we danced very dirty.

I started to kiss her neck and she moaned with pleasure, so I took the opportunity to grab her big titties to massaged them properly. Heather's hot body drove me wild with passion. She took one of my hands and put it on her pussy. I massaged her pussy and big tits at the same time, oh my god I was in love already and we just met.

Heather turned back around held me tight and asked me if I wanted to penetrate her white pussy with my big black cock tonight. I said I would love to penetrate you tonight. Heather said come with me. I want you to meet someone special to me.

Heather took me to the bar to meet another pretty blonde. She said this is my wife Heidi, she is full lesbian and I'm bisexual. I said pleasure to meet you, Heidi. She said pleasure to meet you too, I don't mind if Heather wants you to come home with us to fuck. Heather said she is cool she lets me have some cock on the side and I want you to be my lover.

I said I would love to be your lover. Heidi said since your good with us lets go home and have some fun. I followed the goddesses to their home. It was a very nice big house. I park behind them and walk to their car as Heather opened the door. I took her hand and she smiled at me.

Heidi said I guess chivalry isn't dead after all smiling at me. We entered the house and went straight to the bedroom. Heather said Heidi wants to watch her wife get fucked for the first time by a man, I hope you don't mind. I said I don't mind her watching us make love.

Heather took her dress, bra and panties off and got into bed. I took my belt off dropped it on the ground, I took my shirt off then I took my pants off.

Both Heather and Heidi were looking at my erection and I fucking loved it more than they could ever know.

Heidi said wow that's a big black cock no wonder you chose to fuck him tonight. Heather said oh yeah when I felt his huge cock at the club I almost died of pleasure. I smiled at her climbing on the bed. I spread her sweet white thighs and began to lick her pink slit up and down. The goddess Heather was delicious, I started chewing on her clit and fingering her pussy. She held my head and thoroughly enjoyed it.

Then she said my turn after a while. Heather stroked my cock and licked my cock head. Heidi took her dress off, then her bra and panties to watch us. Heather blew my mind as she sucked me with expert skill that I couldn't believe. I said lay back goddess. I want to penetrate you as your wife watches.

Heather laid back spread her sweet white thighs. I entered her forcefully. She moaned as I started pumping my black dick in and out of her pussy. I said damn Heather this some tight ass white pussy, *feels so good on my cock. Heather said your big cock feels even better in my pussy. I squeezed her big tits and fucked her hard. Heather squealed and gave up the orgasm, lubricating my whole cock with cream. I said bend over sweet cheeks, I entered her doggie and pulled her hair. I rammed her doggie as Heidi watched rubbing her pussy.*

Heather moaned looking back at me. I pulled her long blonde hair and pounded her properly. I saw more cream coat my cock and I knew she came again. I laid down and I told Heather to ride me goddess. She said with pleasure as she mounted me and slid down my full erection. I squeezed her big tits as she fucked me. Heather looked at me and her wife smiling enjoying my cock massaging her pussy.

Heather moaned oh Heidi as she came again on my cock. I couldn't hold my pleasure anymore, so I let myself ejaculate my warm sperm inside of sweet Heather. I smacked her big booty and said damn that was great. Heather said tell me about it, I loved it a lot. She leaned down and kissed me then Heidi kissed her wife saying that was hot.

*Heidi was still horny, she crawled over me to get
to Heather. She spread her sweet white thighs
then started licking Heather's pussy as I watched.
I thought is she going to eat my sperm too. I saw it
oozing out of Heather's pussy and she ate it.*

*Heidi looked at me and said your sperm taste good
in Heather's pussy. I said thanks Heidi and she
said you're welcome. Heather said don't worry I
will suck you dry soon. I said I look forward to it.
Heather said bring that pussy over here. Heidi
turned around so that Heather was able to eat her
pussy while she ate the cream out of her pussy. It
was a heavenly vision of them eating each other
until they both came hard. I will never forget it as
long as I live. They kissed and held each other
tight when they were done eating.*

*I held both of their hands as we lay in bed before
we drifted off to sleep. I woke up to the married
couple looking at me with their pretty faces. I said
good morning goddesses and they both giggled.
Heidi said are you still okay with the three of us
being together. I said hell yeah, I'm great, that's
when Heather kissed me.*

Heather said this makes me very happy, you are ok with my wife and me. I said that is wonderful news and Heidi threw the covers off. Heidi said your dick is hard after last night. I said morning boner don't worry you ladies will get used to it.

Heather said I don't like wasting that big boner. She pounced on it and started sucking my dick. I enjoyed it as she sucked harder and harder with Heidi watching. I loved it more and more until I erupted into Heather's warm mouth. She sucked it all down with pleasure, I said wow that was amazing after she swallowed it all.

I said that is wake up pleasure, feel free to do that anytime you want, and Heidi giggled then said I'll go make us breakfast. Twenty minutes later, breakfast was ready, and we sat down to eat it. That's when I found out that Heidi is a great cook, great scrambled eggs and sausages with tea or coffee.

I scarfed it down quickly and said thank you Heidi, you are a wonderful cook. She said thank you sweetie and your welcome. I hugged and kissed Heather goodbye. Heidi hugged me tight and kissed me on the cheek then said thanks for pleasing my beautiful wife. I said it was my pleasure to please her.

I left their home walking to my Audi A8, I couldn't believe my good fortune. I was busy running my software company all week, so I couldn't see Heather and Heidi. Friday night I told Heather that I was free, and she said come over. So, I went over, since I live close to their house.

I rang the doorbell and waited. The door opened and I said there are my two goddesses. They both laughed out loud. Heather hugged and kissed me. Heidi hugged me two. We sat on the couch and talked. Heidi asked what I did for a living that's when I told her that I run my own software company. She said wow impressive, and I said thank you, Heidi.

Heather said that we are both accountants for separate companies. I said cool, you guys count the beans and they laughed. I rubbed Heather's sweet white thighs and said I missed you all week. Heather said I missed you too stud. Heidi said I missed you too honey. I hugged her and kissed her

on the lips, I missed you too Heidi and she smiled.
Heather said your first kiss from a man, steamy.
Heidi turned red, I said sorry, and Heidi said its ok
I just wasn't expecting it. Heather said I liked it
and Heidi said I liked it too smiling.

Heather said can you stay the whole weekend. I
said of course there is nowhere else I'd rather be
than here with you two pretty ladies. Heather said
I'm glad and happy to hear that babe. We as a
triple went shopping in Austin, Texas for the first
time. People were staring at us with immense
jealousy as we shopped. I brought my two
goddesses anything that they wanted and more.

Heidi was looking at some short skirts and I
bought them for her. She said are you sure I said
yeah, you have a great body, I'm sure Heather
would love you in them. Heather said oh yeah
baby, I would love you in those. I said see we have
the same taste. Heidi said okay, I'll get them.

Heather was looking at some sexy red panties. I
said get those, she said why, I love a woman in red
panties. Heather said I'll take them then I

massaged her big ass saying thanks baby. She kissed me and said you're welcome stud.

I was behind Heidi when she accidentally moved back into me. I held her hips, but it was too late her big ass pancaked my hard cock and I held her. Heidi said oops sorry then she said why is your dick hard again. Heather said it is and grabbed my cock then pressed her big ass into my cock.

I grind my dick into her ass. Heidi said oh my god you two are going to make my pussy wet stop that now. Heather said I can't his big dick always makes me hot. I moaned and people started coming our way. I let go of Heather's hips and she moved away saying we will finish this at home later. We finished shopping packed up Heidi's SUV. Heather and I were in the back seat making out like crazy. She took my dick out and started stroking it. I took her big tits out and sucked them hard.

Heather bent over and I plunged my dick in her. I held her hips and pumped like crazy. Heidi pulled over into a parking lot to watch us fuck. She said I guess you guys couldn't wait until we got home huh. Heather said I hate wasting a boner. I fucked her harder and she spilled her cream on my pole as Heidi watched. I gave her more and more dick until I gave up my warm sperm to her tight pink slit.

Months into our relationship with Heather and Heidi. I told Heather that I wanted to fuck Heidi. She said go for it, but I don't think she will let you fuck her. I said leave that to me. Heather said ok. I was asleep between Heather and Heidi. I was horny and ready, so I spooned Heidi with my erection and felt up her big titties kissing her neck just like Heather does all the time.

I rubbed her clit and fingered her pussy. I couldn't believe that she didn't stop me. When I was sure that she was super wet I forced my dick quickly into her pussy balls deep. Heidi said oh my god you're in the wrong hole. Heather laughed out loud oops, his dick is in you turning on the light.

I said relax Heidi don't be so uptight, just enjoy. I started sliding in and out of her pussy. I said damn Heidi this some fine pussy. Heather giggled *and Heidi said enjoy yourself this is just a onetime thing. I held her tight so she wouldn't get away. I was fucking her good when she moaned. I felt Heidi lubricating my cock and I said did you cum. Heidi said no I didn't, Heather looked and said I see cream. Heidi said fine, your big dick made me cum. I said oh yeah, I made hot Heidi cream. She said whatever shut up and fuck me.*

I pounded the shit out of Heidi, she came a few more times as I gave it to her good. I was about to cum when she said don't come in me, I'm not on birth control like Heather. I moaned and said sorry Heidi as I filled her up with my sperm. Heidi said oh my god I hope I don't get pregnant you horny bastard. I said I'm sorry Heidi I've always wanted to fuck you and come in your tight pussy.

Heather said its true he told me he wanted to fuck you, but I told him you wouldn't let him. He got that pussy congratulations. I said I'll take care of both of you if you get pregnant. I'll never leave you ladies. Heidi said that's great to hear, she kissed me and said thanks for the orgasms. I said my pleasure.

Heather said I'm sorry but I hope you get pregnant. I want a baby to make us four a family. Heidi said oh wow I never knew you wanted a baby. Heather said I kept quiet because you said you didn't want kids. But when my boyfriend said he wanted to fuck you; my hope grew out of control. Heather said please don't be mad wifey. I love you and Heidi said I love you too. Then Heidi said I hope I get pregnant too. I said I love both of you and their eyes got big. Heidi kissed me more passionately than before and Heather kissed the hell out of me too.

Three months later, Heidi was pregnant with my baby and Heather was happy as shit, so was I at the prospect of a baby. Six months later when Abigail was born, the three of us were proud parents. We hire nanny Holly to take care of baby Abigail when we were at work. I moved in with Heather and Heidi when the baby was born. We had to explain our relationship to Holly.

Heidi said once upon a time, Heather had a horny boyfriend who desired her wife, so they conspired to get his big black cock deep in my white pussy. The horny boyfriend ejaculated his baby making sperm into me when I told him not too, 9 months later I gave birth and here we are now. I said for the record she had like 5 orgasms when I entered the wrong hole by accident. Heidi said his big dick would give any bitch an orgasm, it's a true pleasure stick. I said thank you Heidi by hugging and kissing her lovingly.

Holly said that is one steamy tale of lust. Holly looked at my crotch, I wondered if she was wet too. Later that night in bed, I asked Heather if I could bone the nanny. She said go for it sweetie, I don't mind. Heidi said what are you two conspiring about over there. Heather said he wants to bang the nanny. Heidi said she is on birth control.

I said that is great news to my horny ears. Both of them laughed out loud. A few weeks later, Holly was in the laundry room when I saw her wearing short sexy little dress. I came up behind her and hugged her tight kissing her neck with my boner glued to her big ass. I said hello Holly, how are you doing today. She giggled and said I'm fine boss. I felt up her big melons and Holly moaned oh boss, I didn't know that you wanted me.

I said I want you badly Holly, she said what about Heather and Heidi. I said I told them I want you and they said go for it. Holly said in that case lets fuck, I've always wanted some black in me. I said that's my girl, I saw you look at my crotch when Heidi told the story. Holly turned around and we French kissed each other with a lot of lust and passion. Holly undid my pants and it dropped to the ground. She took my dick out and went to her knees. She put my dick in her mouth and started sucking.

I held onto the watching machine for dear life as Holly sucked the hell out of my cock. I pulled her up and bent her over the washing machine. I pulled up her dress and moved her panties to the side. I slammed my cock up her cunt and started fucking her like mad. I held her hips and fucked the shit out of Holly as she screamed with pleasure.

She moaned oh god boss your dick is so big and it's making me cum again. I pulled her hair and really gave it to her good. I smacked her ass and punished her pussy properly until I had enough and let myself go inside her pink hole. I massaged and smacked her juicy ass. She turned around and kissed me, she said your hard-black cock inside my white pussy was so good, thank you for wanting me.

Heidi said how was it Holly and we both jumped being surprised. Heather giggled and said how was it, Holly. Holly said it was great I thoroughly enjoyed his big dick and all the wonderful orgasms it produced. I said I'm happy that you are pleased.

Heidi said can eat the cum out of your pussy and Heather replied me too. Holly said sure but I'm not returning the favor, I love men. Heather and Heidi said deal. Holly sat on the dishwasher and spread her sweet white thighs. Heidi ate my cream out of her pussy then Heather said same some for me. Heidi stopped eating and let Heather eat Holly's pussy. Holly held both of their heads and enjoyed the tongue lashing while looking at me smiling.

I said oh god this is so fucking hot I can't stand it. The baby monitor went off and Holly said sorry ladies I have to go now, she pulled down her dress and fixed her panties then ran upstairs. Heidi looked at me strange then knelt before me. I said

*what are you doing, she said I want to try and suck
you dry. Heather does it all the time and it looks
fun.*

*I said cool go for it, I was already hard from
watching the licking. Heather instructed her how
to please me and Heidi started doing a great job. I
enjoyed it as she sucked me harder and harder.
When I felt my orgasm, I felt free to let it go into
Heidi's mouth, and she swallowed it all. She
smiled at me and said thanks for letting me try, I
know I'm not as good as Heather. I said you were
great, and you made me cum then you swallowed.*

*Heidi's phone rang, she said oh my god it's my
mother. Heather said answer it see what she
wants, Heidi answered saying hi mom what's up,
all I heard is that is not right to keep a baby from
its grandmother. What is her name, Heidi said her
name is Abigail? Then I heard when can I see her.
Heidi looked at Heather and she said next
weekend.*

*The week went by quickly and we packed up the
baby and nanny Holly. We drove to Heidi's mom's
house. We rang the bell; we were greeted*

enthusiastically by Heidi's mom Hope. Holly gave baby Abigail to her grandmother. It was a beautiful sight of a doting grandmother of her granddaughter. We went inside the house and sat on the couch. Hope said I cannot thank you enough for giving me a grandbaby.

I said my pleasure Hope that's when I noticed that Heidi's mom hope was fine as hell. I noticed her big tits and fat ass that she gave to Heidi. Hope showed us to our rooms. We put our stuff away.

We let Hope spend as much time with the baby as possible. Which gave us a break from baby duties. Holly didn't mind one bit; Hope even had a crib which was Heidi's when she was a baby. Hope put baby Abigail down for the evening with Holly without any trouble.

We all got ready for bed; I went to the kitchen to get some water that is when I ran into Hope in the kitchen. She hugged me tight with her amazing body saying thanks for giving her a granddaughter. I said my pleasure Hope, I see where Heidi gets her hot body from. Hope turned red and said you charmer.

Hope kissed me on the cheeks and said you have a good night. I said you too sweet Hope and she giggled walking away. Her ass looked amazing jiggling away. It was a wonderful weekend visiting Heidi's mom.

We left and went home after a lot of hugging and crying. Hope said please visit again. Heidi said we will mom. We were home and settled back into our routines. One morning I came down for breakfast. Holly was with the baby; it was Heather and Heidi cooking as I walked in. I said good morning Heather. I hugged Heidi from behind with my morning boner. I said how is the world's sexiest baby mama. Heidi said I know what you are doing and it's not going to work. Heather laughed out loud that's not going to stop him from trying to knock you up again.

A few months later, I was in bed with Heather and Heidi. I said we should sleep naked. Heather said great idea and took off her night gown. Heidi said what the hell, you've seen me naked, fucked me and knocked me up. She took off her baby doll nightgown. I took my boxers off and Heidi said damn boy you are always hard and ready for pussy. I said I want Heidi's sweet white pussy and Heather laughed out loud.

Heidi's said you are never going to give up are you. Heather said nope. Heidi said very well get on top and give it to me. I hope I don't get pregnant this time. I jumped on her quickly before she changed her mind. I kissed Heidi and Heather moaned I love watching you two. I penetrated Heidi deep and started pounding her pussy with passion and vigor. She held me tight as I fucked her silly. I said damn Heidi this some fine ass pussy. She giggled and said your unbelievable.

I felt her body vibrate and I knew she came. I bent her over and said I've always wanted you doggie. I smacked her big ass and took her from behind. I moaned oh Heidi I love fucking your tight ass pussy. She moaned and gave up the cream as I pounded her properly. Heidi said maybe I should give it up to you more. Heather said really now I would love that more than my boyfriend. I said not likely.

I moaned and filled Heidi with my cream and I told her that I love you Heidi. She said I love you too my baby daddy. Heather said I love him too and I said I love you more Heather. Three months later Heather was pregnant again. Heather was happy again, we told Hope the good news. She told us that she won the lottery and told us to come over this weekend because she had a present for us.

So, we went over that weekend with the baby and Holly. Hope took us out to the back of her estate and there was a brand-new house. She said this is yours Heidi. Heidi said wow really thank you mom. Hope said it has six bedrooms, three upstairs and three downstairs, you guys can live here if you like.

Heidi said we will think long and hard about this and make a decision. A month later we decided to move into the new house and sell the one we are living in. Holly moved in with us too, baby Abigail keeps her very busy and we pay her pretty well.

Five months later when baby Andy was born, Hope was very happy to be closer to us. She was over all the time to see her grandchildren. We were happy to see her too. Holly was busy as hell with the two kids. I found time to bone Holly to keep her sanity.

Hope gave us a break by watching both grandkids with Holly. Holly really appreciated it a lot. One night we put the kids to bed over at Hope's house with Holly. Holly and I took a nap on the couch then we woke up. Hope wasn't around. Holly said I miss us fucking. I said I miss fucking you too baby. I kissed Holly and jumped on her sexy ass. She undid my pants quickly and I shoved my dick in her horny vagina. She held me tight and said oh my god I miss your black cock deep in my white pussy.

I gave Holly all the cock she needed, pounding her into the couch. I saw Holly's eyes roll back in her head and she moaned oh god yes creaming my black bone deep in her white cunt. She said your turn give me your warm sperm. I held her shoulders and tore her white pussy up, I felt tightness in her pussy as she came again squeezing my shaft forcing the release of my hot sperm in her cunt. I moaned loudly and gave it up to her.

I kissed Holly and we held each other. Hope said what's this and we both jumped up all naked post coitus. Hope said does Heidi and Heather know about this. I said they both know about this and they are ok with this. Hope said wow you are fucking my daughter, Heather and the nanny.

I said yeah, Holly said I better go. She left Hope and me alone. She said I watched you fuck the nanny and she liked it. I said it turns me that you watched me fuck Holly the nanny.

Hope was looking at my cock and when I became hard again, she said wow your hard again and you just fucked the nanny. I said I'm very horny all the time. I need to fuck a lot. Hope said have you ever thought about fucking an older woman. I said yeah when I saw your body. Hope smiled at me, I said I love your nightgown, it's very translucent.

Hope said sorry I didn't mean to turn you on. I said I don't mind being turned on by a beautiful woman. I got up and hugged Hope with my erection. Hope moaned with pleasure and said would you like to sleep in my bed tonight. I said yes, I would love to sleep in your bed tonight.

I massaged her ass and kissed her lips. I said let's go to your bedroom. When we arrived at her bedroom. Hope was very ready for cock. She dropped her night gown then laid back in her bed. She said fuck me with your dirty cock, I'm wet spreading her sweet white thighs. I said oh yeah mounted her and plunging my love dagger into her heart of pleasure. I kissed Hope and began our journey of pleasure together. I gave Hope deep unending pleasure in our lustful embrace. She lubricated my love dagger many times as I pleasured her. I couldn't hold my lust for Hope anymore and I filled her with my love. Hope said wow that was amazing, young studs do know what they are doing in bed. I said I do; I don't know about the rest of them. Hope giggled and said thanks for taking care of me tonight. I said my pleasure and I would do it again if you wish. Hope said I would like that a lot.

We went to sleep holding hands and we were both woken up by Heidi. She said oh my god mom, I didn't know you like black men too. Hope said oh my god I'm so embarrassed. Heidi said don't be embarrassed mom, his huge cock is very persuasive. Hope said tell me about it, I saw him fucking the nanny and suddenly I had to have it. Heidi said like mother like daughter, he fucked me by accident then I let him willingly fuck me again giving you your second grandbaby. Hope said oh my and Heidi said look his cock is hard again.

The end

www.ingramcontent.com/pod-product-compliance
Lightning Source LLC
Chambersburg PA
CBHW060932130726
48001CB00006B/2536